The TEACUP Story

Story written by unknown author
Illustrations by Mary Catherine Webb
Edited by Patricia Canini & Christopher V Webb

The Teacup Story is dedicated to
every person that is
put on the Potter's Wheel
to become a vessel of purpose
and beauty for God and for man.

Yield to the Potter's hand!

Preface

Welcome to The Tea Cup Story—an intimate allegory drawn from the timeless verses of Jeremiah. This narrative is a dedicated embrace for those weathering life's trials, a reflection on the Potter's Wheel, and an anthem for the resilient souls navigating the kiln's fiery crucible.

To every reader, past, present, or future, entwined in the journey of becoming, may these pages resonate with the universal dance of transformation. Within this short allegory lies a whispered assurance that, amid life's trials, the hands of the Master Potter are shaping a purpose uniquely yours.

With heartfelt dedication,

Keith and Mary Catherine Webb

A couple walked into an antique shop one fine day.
Sitting high up upon a shelf
SAT A Beautiful magnificent, little
Teacup

They just fell in love with this teacup. They said;
WE'VE GOT TO HAVE THAT!
THEY WERE STANDING AND ADMIRING IT WHEN ALL OF A SUDDEN, THE TEACUP BEGAN TO TALK TO THEM:
You know I haven't always been like this. There was a time when no one would've wanted me!

I was not attractive at all. YOU see there was a time in my life when I was just an old, HARD, GRAY, LUMP of clay.

The Master Potter came along and picked me up one day and he began to "pat" me, re-shape me. And I said,

STOP IT! A-A-A-H DON'T DO THAT WHAT ARE YOU DOING? LEAVE ME ALONE! HELP!

And He simply looked at me and said; "not yet!"

Then he put me on this wheel and began TO SPIN ME AROUND. I GOT SO DIZZY! I COULD HARDLY SEE WHERE I WAS GOING, I WAS LOSING IT! I FELT SICK TO MY STOMACH AND I SAID, "OHHH, GET ME OUT OF HERE!!!"

BUT HE JUST SAID, "not yet!"

The day came when I finally had taken on another shape from all that patting, molding, squeezing, and pinching.

All of a sudden...

He put me into this FURNACE called the first firing. It was so hot in there. OH I couldn't believe how hot it was! I couldn't stand it. I thought I would die in there.

GET ME OUTTA HERE!

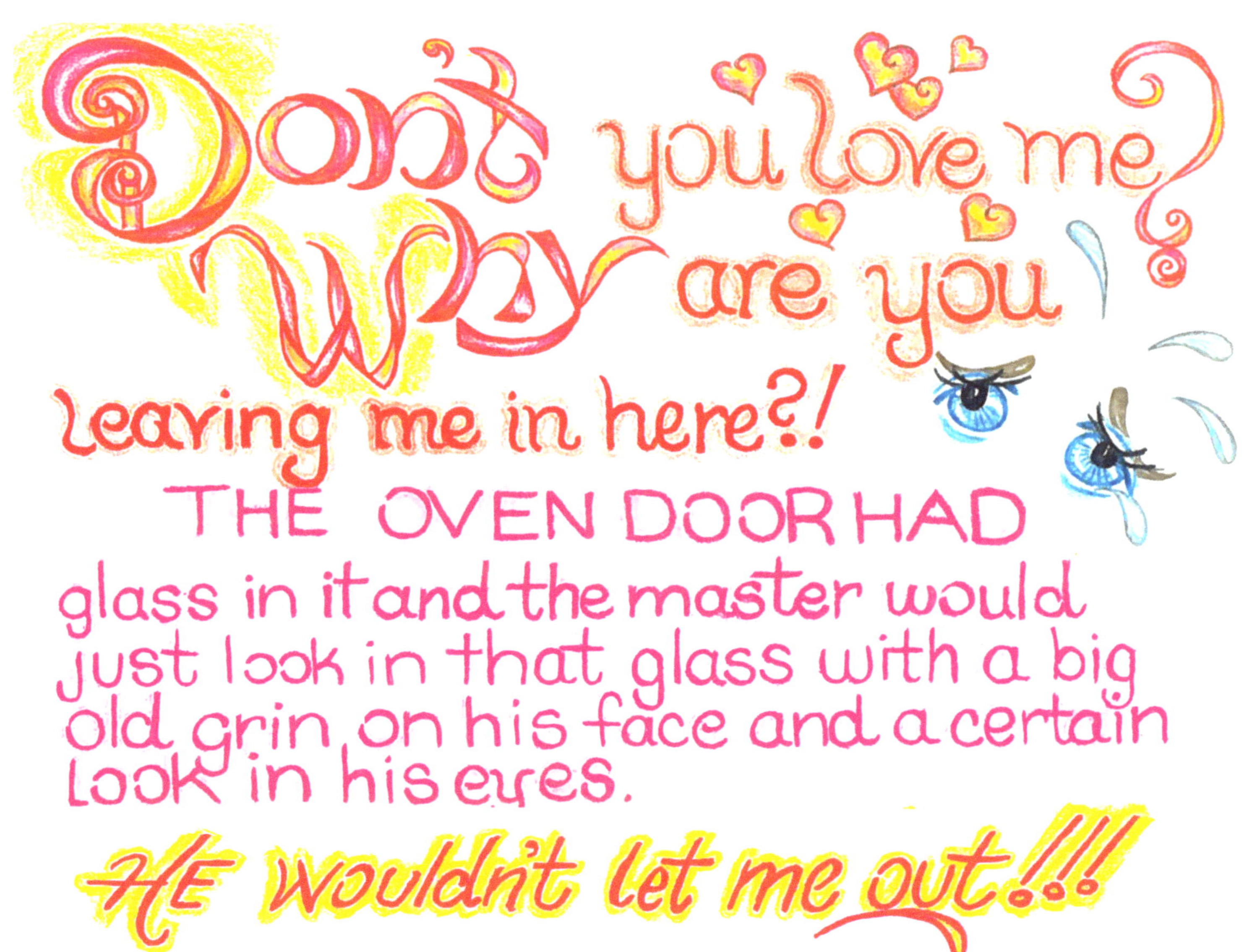
Don't you love me? Why are you leaving me in here?!
THE OVEN DOOR HAD glass in it and the master would just look in that glass with a big old grin on his face and a certain look in his eyes.
HE wouldn't let me out!!!

But he'd just *smile* at me and say... **Not yet!**

Finally! the oven door OPENED and he let me OUT, and I thought SHEW!
Set me on a Shelf
and I thought
Thank God that's over!
THEN he began to PAINT me all over with this stinky paint; changing my color from gray to this to this pretty blue that I am now.
THIS STUFF STINKS!
ITS CHOKING ME!
I DON'T LIKE THIS SMELL!

COUGH!
COUGH!
COUGH!
STOP IT!
STOP IT!
STOP IT!
He'd just say; "NOT YET"!

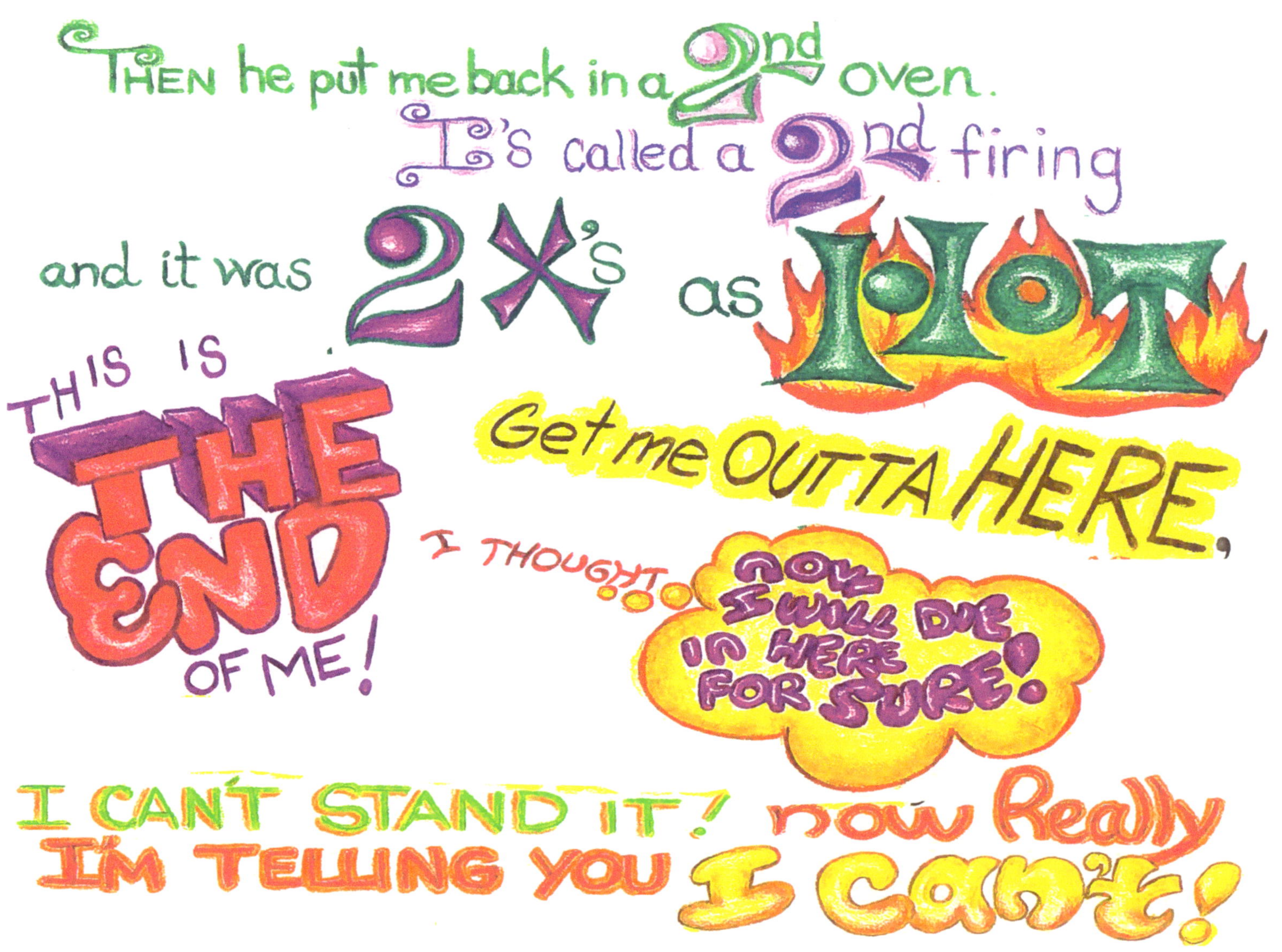

THEN he put me back in a 2nd oven.
It's called a 2nd firing
and it was 2 X's as HOT
THIS IS THE END OF ME!
Get me OUTTA HERE,
I THOUGHT... now I will die in here for sure!
I CAN'T STAND IT! now Really I'M TELLING YOU I can't!

This is gonna KILL me, get me outta here!
He'd just look through that glass and say... Not yet.

Finally, 1 DAY he OPENED the door
and took me UP OUT,
PUT ME HERE on this shelf and let me COOL OFF.
AFTER I HAD COOLED HE CAME BY AND HANDED ME THIS Mirror
I LOOKED AT MYSELF AND COULDN'T BELIEVE HOW I HAD CHANGED...
HOW Beautiful I HAD BECOME
Why—I didn't look anything at all like that old, gray clay that I started out to be

See...
I'm this
Beautiful,
Little,
Delicate
Teacup.
EVERYONE
WANTS
ME
NOW!

There was a time in our life...
when nobody wanted us.
Nobody liked us or paid any attention to us.

They just kicked
us around~
naked
on
us.

But now we're special!
The way you see us now:
wasn't always this way.

WE STARTED FROM
A LUMP OF CLAY!

Group Discussion Questions

Many times the things that attract us have an interesting story behind them. This is also known as a testimony. A testimony is what someone shares about an important experience or season or their life that helped mold them into the person they have become today.

1) Can you think of a testimony or story in your own life?

When we go through times of change in our life before we take a different shape it may begin with a hard or even shocking experience.

2) Is there something that's happened to you that was hard in your life during a time of change that you'd like to share?

Just when you think you're about to come out of a hard place (like the stove in the story), things may get worse!! What goes through your mind when this happens? Do you think "Oh wow! What did I do to deserve this? Did I do something wrong? Or do you think "well maybe I must go through this thing to get to a better place"?

3) What comes to mind in your life that caused great pain only to see later on that it really was for your good?

For Children to ponder:
This is where TRUST is a big deal! It could be your parent's decision to not let you do something or go somewhere or hang out with a certain friend or friends because they love you and can see what you cannot.

4) When was a time that your mom and/or dad did something that was for your own good, but you didn't like it or agree with it?

For Adults to consider :
Perhaps this is where you may wonder if God loves you, why is this happening? Because if He did, why would He allow this to happen? What kind of feelings do you have here? Maybe you have another family member or close friend going through tough times.

5)What do you say or do to encourage them?

(This is a good time to interact with your children so they can see how you navigate your life?)

For Adults to consider :

Perhaps this is where you may wonder if God loves you, why is this happening? Because if He did, why would He allow this to happen? What kind of feelings do you have here? Maybe you have another family member or close friend going through tough times.

5) What do you say or do to encourage them?

(This is a good time to interact with your children so they can see how you navigate your life?)

Finally, you're beginning to climb up and out of a hard place. But unbeknownst to you, you are not completely through with the changes. It's just another phase. You probably will feel disappointed or discouraged or even ANGRY! Remember once again it takes time to finish a good work!

6) What are some ways you can stay on point and not give up ?

Right before the grand finale or big reveal of something wonderful, the hardest part may come first. Just when you think you're not going to make it.

7) What are your choices here?

Can you feel the relief of the Teacup? Finally an end to all the hardships and a wonder-ful reward for all the suffering! Was it worth it? It sure was for that little Teacup. Now we can see how loving the Master Potter truly was! There had to be a process to come to such a beautiful vessel.

8) What would you tell people about such a journey ? Do you have examples to share?

The Master Potter (God) sees us from the beginning to the end. He knows just what it's going to take in time and effort to get you from one place in life to another. Patience, practice, falling down and getting up. It's great to have people in your life to encourage you as you go. Who in your life (a friend or relative) has been there to help you along the way? And who are YOU helping along their way?
We ALL need inspiration from somewhere or someone. The Bible is a great place to find direction and help. Wisdom too! There are many books and movies that share stories of men and women, boys and girls that overcame incredible odds to finish their races and become winners.

9) What are some of the sources you have turned to to get you through life's hard times?

Lastly, The Teacup Story is a simplified illustration of the process one may go through to get to a happy place. YOU have a story IN YOU too because you were created to be a winner!

Bonus

The Teacup Coloring Book

ENJOY COLORING THE TEACUP STORY!!

We recommend placing a piece of cardboard
Between the pages to prevent bleeding through the page

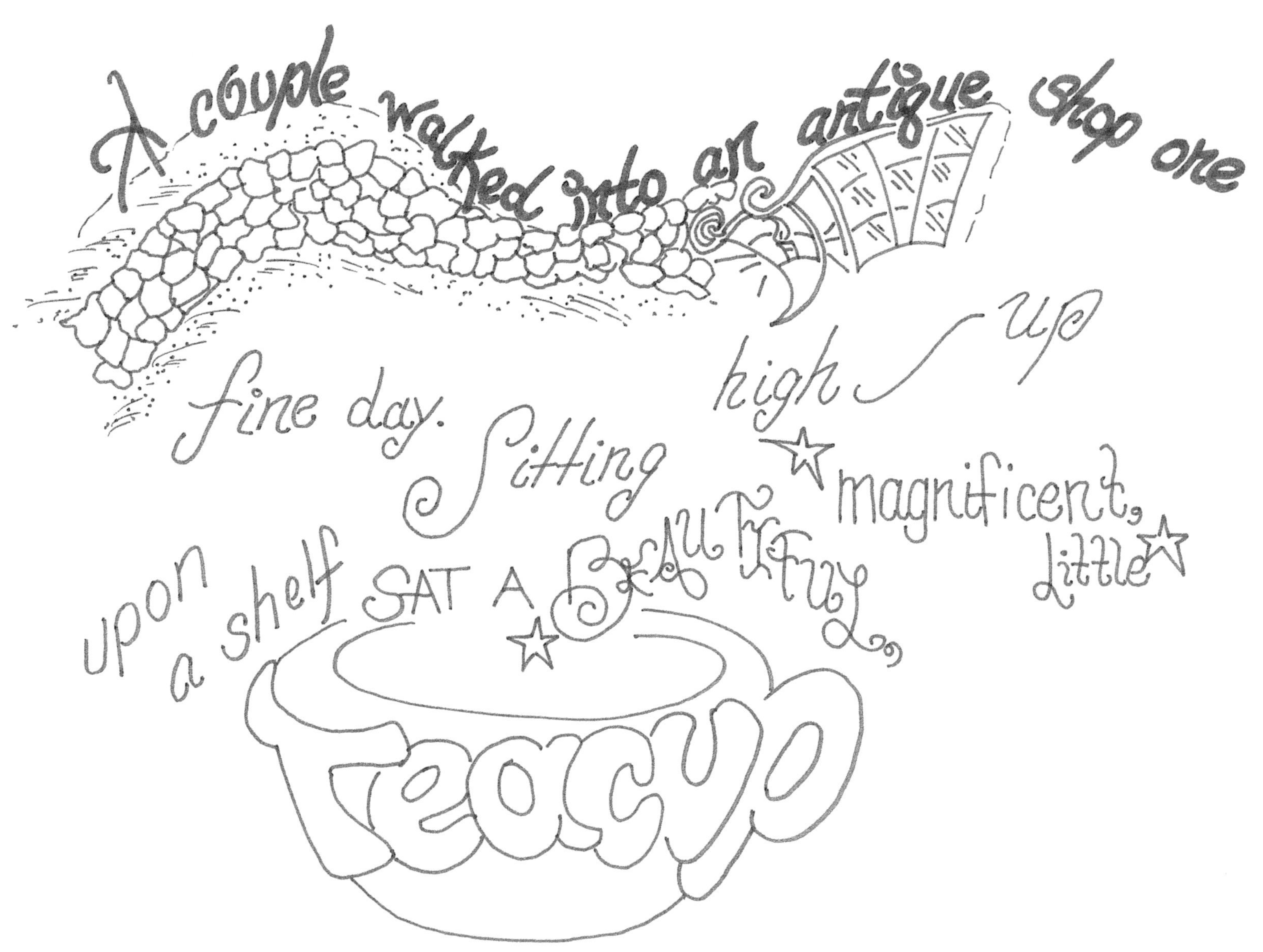

A couple walked into an antique shop one
fine day. Sitting high up
upon a shelf SAT A Beautiful magnificent, little
teacup

They just fell in love with this teacup. They said:
WE'VE GOT TO HAVE THAT!
THEY WERE STANDING AND ADMIRING IT WHEN ALL OF A SUDDEN, THE TEACUP BEGAN TO TALK TO THEM:
YOU KNOW I HAVEN'T ALWAYS BEEN LIKE THIS. THERE WAS A TIME WHEN NO ONE WOULD'VE WANTED ME!

A Time When...

I was not attractive at all. YOU see there was a time in my life when I was just an old, HARD, GRAY, LUMP of clay.

The Master Potter came along and picked me up one day and he began to "pat" me, re-shape me. And I said, STOP IT! A-A-A-A-H DON'T DO THAT WHAT ARE YOU DOING? LEAVE ME ALONE! HELP!

And He simply looked at me and said; "not yet!"

Then he put me on this wheel and he began to spin me around
I was going around more
I was Losin-
it? I felt Sick to my Stomach and I Said - LET ME OFF OF HERE!
BUT HE JUST SAID, "not yet!"
I was spinning around
around and around
so I got Sick so I
I couldn't even see where I was going
around and around

The day came when I finally had taken on another shape from all that patting, molding, squeezing, and pinching. All of a sudden... He put me into this FURNACE called the first firing. It was so hot in there. OH I couldn't believe how hot it was! I couldn't stand it. I thought I would die in there. GET ME OUTTA HERE!

Don't you love me? Why are you leaving me in here?!
THE OVEN DOOR HAD glass in it and the master would just look in that glass with a big old grin on his face and a certain look in his eyes.
HE wouldn't let me out!!!

But he'd just smile at me and say... Not yet!

Finally! the oven door OPENED and he let me OUT, and I thought "SHEW!"
set me on a shelf
Thank God that's over!
THEN he began to PAINT me all over with this stinky paint; changing my color from gray to this to this pretty blue that I am now.
THIS STUFF STINKS!
ITS CHOKING ME!
I DON'T LIKE THIS SMELL!

He'd just say; "NOT YET!"

THEN he put me back in a 2nd oven. It's called a 2nd firing and it was 2 X's as HOT as the first oven.
I THOUGHT... NOW I WILL DIE IN HERE FOR SURE!
THIS WILL FINISH ME OFF.!
THIS IS THE END OF ME!
Get me OUTTA HERE, I CAN'T STAND IT! now Really I'M TELLING YOU I CAN'T!

This is gonna KILL me, get me outta here!
He'd just look through that glass and say... "Not yet."

1 DAY the door Suddenly OPENED and he took me OUT,
PUT ME UP HERE on this shelf and let me COOL OFF.
AFTER I HAD COOLED HE CAME BY AND HANDED ME THIS
I LOOKED AT MYSELF AND COULDN'T BELIEVE HOW I HAD CHANGED...
HOW Beautiful I HAD BECOME!
Why—I didn't look anything at all like that old, gray clay that I started out to be

See...
I'M THIS
Beautiful,
Little,
Delicate
Teacup.
EVERYONE
WANTS
ME
NOW!
PALM
MIRROR CO

There was a time in our life...
when nobody wanted us.
Nobody liked us
or paid any
attention to us.

42

But now we're special!
The way you see us now:
wasn't always this way.

WE STARTED FROM
A LUMP OF CLAY!

About the Author

Embark on a creative journey with Mary Catherine Webb, a seasoned illustrator with a passion that bloomed in her youth. Guided by her mother's artful teachings in drawing women's faces, Mary's artistic endeavors evolved into years of captivating fashion illustration. Drawing and creating are not just skills for Mary; they are expressions of her boundless imagination.

The enchanting tale of the Tea Cup immediately seized Mary's heart upon first hearing it. Driven by a desire to breathe life into this narrative, Mary set out to craft drawings that illuminate the profound connection between the Master Potter and the cup. Despite the original author being unknown, Mary's artistic interpretation adds a new layer of depth and beauty to the story.

Beyond her prowess as an illustrator, Mary is a budding author, weaving tales that come to life through her illustrations. Hailing from the vibrant city of Rockford, Illinois, Mary brings a rich background to her creations. Now residing in Grove City, Ohio, alongside her husband, Keith Webb, Mary continues to be a creative force.

Diving into various projects, Mary and Keith explore realms beyond illustration. From crafting jewelry to designing pinecone decorations and experimenting with alcohol ink art, their collaborative ventures unfold under the artistic umbrella of Nature's Praise. Join Mary Catherine Webb on her artistic odyssey, where each stroke of her pen reveals a new chapter in the captivating world of creativity.

9 798990 419117